D0359633

MAGIC AND THE NIGHT RIVER

Weekly Reader Books presents

MAGIC
AND THE
NIGHT RIVER

by Eve Bunting

Illustrated by Allen Say

Harper & Row, Publishers
New York, Hagerstown, San Francisco, London

This book is a presentation of
Weekly Reader Books.

Weekly Reader Books offers
book clubs for children from
preschool through junior high school.
All quality hardcover books are selected
by a distinguished Weekly Reader Selection Board.

For further information write to:
Weekly Reader Books
1250 Fairwood Ave.
Columbus, Ohio 43216

Magic and the Night River
Text copyright © 1978 by Eve Bunting
Illustrations copyright © 1978 by Allen Say
All rights reserved. No part of this book may be used or
reproduced in any manner whatsoever without written
permission except in the case of brief quotations embodied
in critical articles and reviews. Printed in the United
States of America. For information address Harper & Row,
Publishers, Inc., 10 East 53rd Street, New York, N.Y. 10022.
Published simultaneously in Canada by
Fitzhenry & Whiteside Limited, Toronto.

Library of Congress Cataloging in Publication Data
Bunting, Anne Eve.
    Magic and the night river.

    SUMMARY: A Japanese boy and his grandfather
fish successfully with their cormorants because
they have treated the birds with kindness.
    [1. Fishing—Fiction] I. Say, Allen.
II. Title.
PZ7.B91527Mah   [E]   77-3813
ISBN 0-06-020912-7
ISBN 0-06-020913-5 lib. bdg.

To Ed,
who loves
Birds,
Fishing,
and Me

The cormorants squawked inside their bamboo baskets. Yoshi saw a flash of gray feathers through the webbing, the gleam of a black eye, the curve of a neck. It was important to look and to see everything clearly, because now each night on the river could be the last.

"Ready, Yoshi?" Grandfather asked, and Yoshi nodded.

Together he and his cousins loaded the baskets that held the cormorants onto Grandfather's boat.

The boat did not belong to Grandfather, though he had fished from it for forty years. The boat belonged to Kano, and because it did, half of their nightly catch went to him. Yoshi did not want to think about Kano. Kano was big and strong and he talked with a strong voice.

"Why is it, Yoshi, that your grandfather's boat always brings home the fewest fish?" Kano had asked as they stood on the riverbank. "Is it because your grandfather is now too old? I should rent my boat to a better fisherman. There would be more fish then for me to share."

"There is not anywhere a better master fisherman than Grandfather," Yoshi said fiercely. Kano shrugged.

Yoshi watched Kano load his cormorants onto his second boat. He threw the baskets down carelessly on the deck and the long, narrow boat swayed. Inside one of the baskets a bird screamed its rage.

Yoshi glared at Kano across the water space that divided the two boats. "You should be gentle with the birds," he shouted. "They are easily hurt and they work hard for us."

"Who worries about cormorants?" Kano asked. "The skies are full of cormorants for the taking."

"Grandfather says we owe them kindness. We . . ."

"What do I care what your grandfather says?" Kano sounded angry. "Let him think about other things. Tonight I will be taking careful count of the catch when the fishing is done."

Yoshi glanced quickly at his grandfather.

Grandfather was bent over one of the baskets, his hands moving across it, soothing the birds inside. Old hands with yellowed nails, gentle hands.

Yoshi swallowed. "Shall we ready the sail, Grandfather?" he asked, and Grandfather nodded.

The small breeze tugged at the canvas as Yoshi and his cousin Masa pulled on the ropes. It blew on the lanterns that decorated the barge, on the other side of the river, filled with people who came to watch the fishing. Soon the barge would glide upstream with the working boats. The voices of the people drifted across the darkness and the lanterns spilled their yellow glow on the shine of the water.

Some night I will go on the barge, Yoshi thought. That will be a good thing to do. But he knew he didn't mean it. To watch from the barge would be nothing. Here, with Grandfather, he was a part of everything. A fisherman, fishing on the great river.

Grandfather gave the signal and Yoshi's older cousin, Take, whose place was in the stern, poled their boat away from shore.

The other four boats pushed off too, fanning across the river, their sails opening themselves to the wind.

And there was only the contented sucking of the water, the ripple of the wind in the canvas, the splashing of the polers on the barge. The sounds of the night river. Remember them, Yoshi told himself. Remember them for always.

Grandfather raised a hand and Yoshi knew it was time. He stared down into the dark water. There was nothing to see, but he knew it must be time.

He heard the scraping of the match and saw his grandfather hold its light to the wood in the iron cradle that hung out from the bow. The dry wood took the fire immediately, crackling and spitting. Smoke blew back, rising and drifting to the sky where the night stars hung. It was time.

One by one the bow fires blazed in the other boats.

Yoshi sniffed at the pine smoke. Who will light the first fire when Grandfather is gone, he wondered. He wanted to shout to Kano, "It is Grandfather who knows where the fish lie waiting. He has been lighting the first fire for forty years. Doesn't that mean something?" But he didn't shout anything because all Kano cared about was counting the catch when the fishing was ended. He helped his cousin Masa take down the sails and mast.

They drifted slowly, pulled only by the river. The light from the fires danced on the water, calling the fish from the depths to where the birds could reach them. There was a hiss and a shower of sparks as a piece of burning wood fell into the river.

Across the water the bargemen raised their poles. Yoshi saw the drops hanging like pearls from the poles, saw the blur of people's faces behind the railing.

"Should I release the birds now, Grandfather?" he asked, and Grandfather nodded.

Yoshi felt the simmer of excitement that came to him the same way each night. It was time.

He took from the box the wedges of wood with the cords wrapped around them. Then he opened the first basket and felt under the half-raised lid. His hand found Itchi-ban, their number-one cormorant, and eased it out. The ring around its neck gleamed silver and red, reflecting the flames. Quickly Yoshi passed the cord around the bird's breast and tied it.

"Grandfather?" he said, holding the bird toward the old man.

Grandfather leaned forward and touched the cormorant's head once. It was this way each night, with each bird. The old hands reaching out, warm and gentle.

"Go," he said, and Yoshi held on to the end of the cord and set the cormorant free.

The first second of flight was only a flurry of awkward wings. Then Itchi-ban surged away, the air thick about it, its body beating against the dark, the feel of life on a leash, spinning, cartwheeling to dive, crashing into the river.

Yoshi passed the cord to Grandfather. His smile answered his grandfather's smile. We know, he thought. We feel together. It could not be this way for his cousins, who handled only the boat and not the birds. The strength of his feeling was almost an embarrassment, and he was glad to lean over and bring out the second bird.

Soon all the cormorants were in the air, swooping and diving, filling the night with their wings and their hoarse cries.

Fourteen birds.

Grandfather handled eight from the bow. He held the cords between his fingers, shifting them to the birds' needs.

Yoshi worked only six. He had not yet the skill to manage more.

Once Grandfather had been master of twelve birds. His fingers had moved so quickly then that to watch him was to watch a juggler at work. Now the fingers were bent and stiff.

"Fourteen birds for two handlers," Kano had said. "Am I a fool to rent my boat to two such fishermen?"

Yoshi remembered his words as he jiggled his cords. "Come on," he whispered. "Dive for us. Bring us back fish, fish, fish."

His grandfather reeled in one bird, its neck bulging with the fish it had caught but could not swallow. Grandfather held the cormorant's beak over a basket and ran his hand along its neck. The big fish spilled in a stream of silver from the bird's throat. Grandfather nodded toward Yoshi's cord. "Yours," he said.

Yoshi pulled in his fisher cormorant and stripped its throat into his waiting basket. When he had first come with Grandfather he had known little and had had to ask many questions.

"Why does the ring around the throat not choke the bird, Grandfather?"

"Because it is placed there with delicacy. It is tight enough so that the cormorant cannot swallow the big fish, yet it is loose enough for the small ones to slip down. That way the bird is happy because it is not hungry. And we are happy too, Yoshi, because with the big fish to sell we are not hungry either."

"Pay attention to your cords, my Yoshi," Grandfather called now, and Yoshi nodded.

On the next boat, Kano was reeling in. His cormorants fought and pecked at each other, hanging in the air beside the boat, held tight on short lines. Too tight, Yoshi thought. Even I know better than to hold the lines like that.

Grandfather's birds were working well. Time and again they came with their catches and flapped away to fish again. Do they know how much we need a good catch tonight? Yoshi wondered.

The air was alive with the birds' cries and screams as the river was alive with their lights and shadows. Do they know? Yoshi wondered.

There was a flurry of work on all the boats. Once Kano shouted across, "We have one basket almost filled, old man. How goes it with you?"

Grandfather said nothing.

It was then that one of the other boats bumped theirs. Yoshi had seen this happen before, here where the river ran swift and narrow. But he'd never seen what happened next. One of the men on the other boat stumbled. His hands lost control of his lines and they tangled with the lines of another.

Now all the boats were nudging, brushing sides, and the birds were too close, flying in a jumble, their cords tangling.

A rustling, like a small wind, came from the watchers on the barge.

The birds squawked their rage, spinning in furious circles, almost strangling one another. The cords were a great shadowy cobweb that hung above the dark gleam of the river, the birds darting through it like monstrous flies caught in its maze. Yoshi tried to let his eyes follow the lines that ran from his fingers. Where was Itchi-ban? Which were their cormorants? If they would only stay still!

Panic urged the birds to greater struggle. One plummeted into the river, the cord a cocoon around its body. One hung upside down, the cord twisted on its neck. One dangled by a wingtip, its other wing flapping weakly.

Yoshi's throat felt tight, as if he too wore a metal ring.

"Grandfather?" he asked, and his grandfather nodded. It was the way it always was between them, the meaning clear without words spoken. Slowly Yoshi unclenched his hands and let the cords hang free.

A bird lifted itself from the web, screeching loudly, its line trailing behind it. Another pulled loose. Its cord caught but the bird jerked and its wings pushed away the night as it rose to freedom.

Grandfather looked unblinkingly at Yoshi. Then he spread his fingers wide and stood motionless, his face turned to the sky.

Good-bye birds, Yoshi thought. We will not need you again. There was a terrible sadness in him as he watched their cormorants skim away into the shadows. It was as though everything he and his grandfather had had together went with them. He rubbed the smoke sting from his eyes. Good-bye birds. May kindness find you.

On the other boat Kano cursed and twitched his lines.

The men stepped from boat to boat, changing places as they tried to unravel the quivering web.

On Grandfather's boat there was only calm.

The cousins had pulled in their poles.

Grandfather sat quietly in the bow. He lit his pipe from a burning log. Sparks flew around his face and died to blackness before they touched the water.

What is he thinking? Yoshi wondered. Does he remember all the years on the boat? The fish he's taken? The birds he's known?

There was a sudden flurry of dark wings, a scrabble of clawed feet on the deck.

Yoshi gasped.

Itchi-ban was perched on the gunwale by the fish basket. Its eyes held no fear as Yoshi crept toward it.

Grandfather knocked the embers from his pipe into the river and smiled.

"Take what it offers us," he said, and Yoshi took the bird and emptied the fish from its throat.

He held Itchi-ban's warmth close against him. Should he put it back in its basket? Fasten tight the lid? Slowly he opened his hands and set it free.

A second bird came back, and a third.

Yoshi was dizzy with excitement. He and Masa and Grandfather worked together, taking the gifts the cormorants brought, releasing them to fish again.

Who could believe it? Grandfather had no need of cords to hold his birds. They were held to him by something stronger.

Their baskets bulged with the shine of their catch. The bargemen poled the barge closer so the people could see.

Kano shook his head and watched with amazement. Then he opened *his* hands and let his birds go. But his birds did not return.

Grandfather's baskets were full. Fish tumbled over their tops to wriggle back into the river.

"Shall we fish for you now, Kano?" Grandfather asked.

"No," Kano said.

"We are ready to go back then." Yoshi did not try to hide his joy. "We will wait for you on the riverbank."

He counted thirteen of their cormorants perched on the gunwales, waiting, and Itchi-ban standing proudly on the overhanging prow. All of their birds had returned. Yoshi watched as Grandfather gathered them one by one and placed them in their baskets. Tonight he was content to leave this job to Grandfather alone. He saw how Grandfather fondled the head of each bird before he closed the lid. Old hands with yellowed nails, gentle hands. He had left Itchi-ban till last. Grandfather held the big bird close. Yoshi saw his lips move but he could not hear the whispered words. Then Itchi-ban too was settled into its basket.

"The old man has magic," Kano said, and there was a new sound to his voice.

Yoshi smiled. It might be that Kano would never understand what kind of magic had brought the birds back. For now there were other matters to think about as Masa and Take poled the boat toward home. Grandfather could train new birds. He could have eight on cords and others working free. With Yoshi's six their cormorants would bring in many fish. Kano would like that.

Grandfather seemed to creak as he bent to examine the night's catch.

His strength grows less each day, Yoshi thought. But my strength grows greater. It is another kind of magic. Together we will have many nights on the night river.

Format by Kohar Alexanian
Set in 12 pt. Times Roman
Composed by Royal Composing Room, Inc.

HARPER & ROW, PUBLISHERS, INC.